This edition first published in 2017 by Book Island
info@bookisland.co.uk

Original title: *Trīs draugi vienas upes krastā*
© 2014 *liels un mazs*, Latvia
Text © 2014 Inese Zandere
Adaptation of the story by Lawrence Schimel
Translation by Sabīne Ozola
Illustrations © 2014 Juris Petraškevičs

British Library Cataloguing-in-Publication Data
A CIP record for this title is available from the British Library.

Edited by Frith Williams
Typeset by Vida & Luke Kelly, New Zealand
Printed in Latvia on FSC certified paper
ISBN: 978-1-911496-06-9

Teacher notes for this title are available from www.bookisland.co.uk.

Visit www.bookisland.co.uk for more information about our books.

This edition wouldn't have been possible without the generous support of

Kultūras ministrija

Latvija 1OO ▬▬

Latvijas Rakstnieku savienība

A tale by **Inese Zandere**
adapted by Lawrence Schimel

One House for All

Illustrated by **Juris Petraškevičs**

BOOK ISLAND

Once upon a time, three good friends —
Raven, Crayfish, and Horse —
came together under a tall tree
in a green meadow
on the bank of a river.

All three were now grown-up
and wanted to get married,
but they also wanted to remain close.

So the three friends decided to build a big new house
where they, their wives, and their children

'What will our house look like?'
Raven wanted to know.
'Let's design one!' said Horse.

Crayfish immediately picked up a stick.
Holding it firmly in his claws,
he began to draw a house
in the sand on the riverbank.

'It needs to have a wide door
leading down to a long passage
three claw spans under the water,'
Crayfish said.

The next to take the stick was Horse.
'It should have a large, green living room
with juicy grass, at least three acres big,'

Then it was Raven's turn to use the stick.
'It should have a luxurious bedroom
on top of a tree that's three metres tall,'
Raven declared.

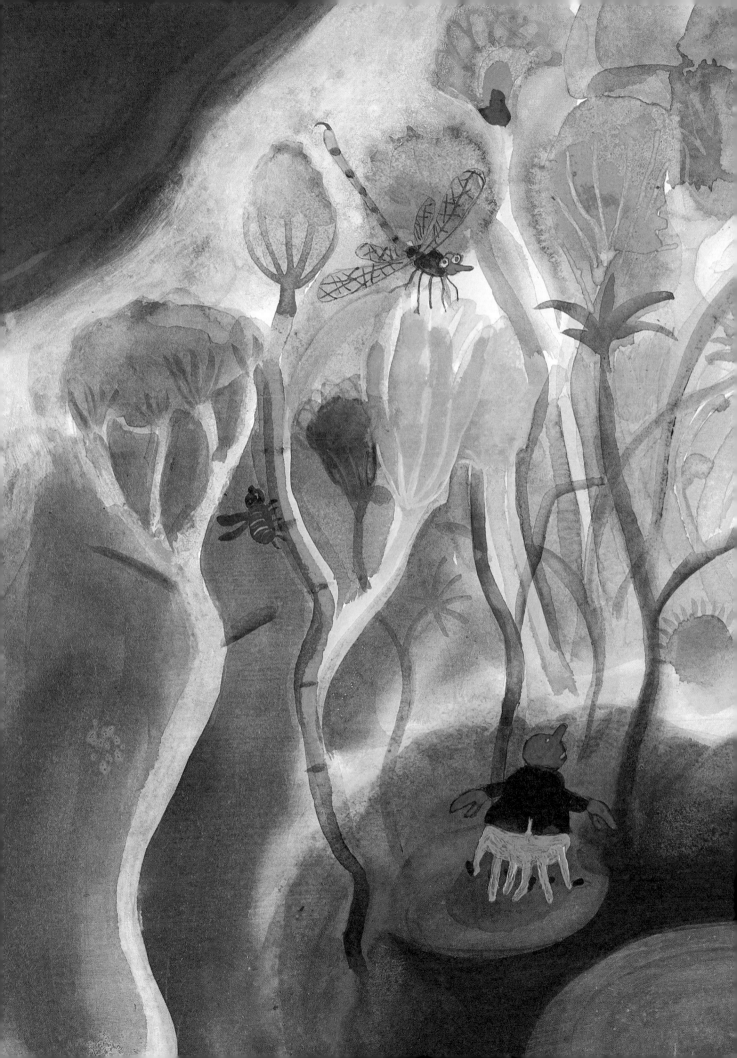

Now the three friends
took a close look
at the three drawings.

'My wife and children
can't possibly run around
in a meadow,'
Crayfish complained.

'My wife and children
can't possibly go in the water,'
Raven worried.

'My wife and children
won't be able to fly to the bedroom,'
Horse realised.

The three friends sat down by the river
feeling very upset.

Each of them had drawn a house
that would be perfect for their own families,
but not at all suitable for the others.

'Does this mean we shouldn't
get married at all?'
Crayfish wondered.

'Maybe we shouldn't
get married at all!'
Raven exclaimed.

'... not get married at all ...'
said Horse thoughtfully.

Silence fell.
Only the river babbled on,
interrupting the three friends' thinking.
An hour passed, then another, and a third,
but the three friends were still thinking.

'Why should my wife and children need to fly?
They are horses. They'll live in a meadow,'
Horse said at last.

'Why should my wife and children
need to go in the water?
They are ravens.
They'll live in a tree,'
said Raven.

'Why should my wife and children
need to run in a meadow?
They are crayfish.
They'll live in the river,'
Crayfish declared.

'I have a solution!'
Crayfish shouted.
'We can all live together
in one big house
with three different floors!'

'Of course, that's what we'll do!'
cried Raven.
'Our families will live on different floors
in a three-storey house!'

'That's just what we'll do!'
Horse agreed.

And in the evenings,
they all sat together by the river
swinging their legs:
two legs if they were ravens,
four legs if they were horses,
and lots of legs if they were crayfish.